SNOW DUDE

Words and Pictures by

Daniel Kirk

Hyperion Books for Children
New York

Nick and Kara Candlewick
were working very hard
to build a funny snow dude
in their own backyard.

"I wish that he could talk,"
said Nick. "I wish that he could run!"
"We could chase him," Kara said,
"and have a lot of fun!"

"Be careful," cried a gust of wind.
"Be careful what you say,
for there's a little mischief
in the chilly air today!"

Nick popped in a carrot nose,
and Kara poked some eyes.
Suddenly, the snow dude grinned
and stamped his feet. "Surprise!"

He said, "I'm a snow dude,
as wild as wild can be.
Run as fast as you can run—
you won't catch up with me!"

The snow dude leaped, and hollered, *"Whooooo!"*
and raced around the block.
He dashed right past a couple
who were shoveling their walk.

"Stop! Please, stop!" the woman said.
"For it would bring us joy
if you would come to live with us,
and be our little boy!"

He answered, "I'm a snow dude,
as wild as wild can be.
Run as fast as you can run—
you won't catch up with me!"

The snow dude jumped and skipped and hopped
along the icy street.
He sped down to the heart of town,
on little snow-dude feet.

He hurried by the bakery—
past cookies, cakes, and bread.
The baker stuck her nose outside,
and this is what she said:

"Wait! I want to talk to you!
I can't believe my eyes,
but I could use a boy like you
to help me cool my pies!"

He answered, "I'm a snow dude,
as wild as wild can be.
Run as fast as you can run—
you won't catch up with me!"

He dashed right past a van
with CIRCUS painted on its side.
"Stop!" the lion tamer said.
"Come on, let's take a ride!

"Your future's in the big top—
I can really take you far!
Come with me, I guarantee
that I'll make you a star!"

He answered, "I'm a snow dude,
as wild as wild can be.
Run as fast as you can run—
you won't catch up with me!"

He scurried and he hurried
by the entrance to the zoo,
past polar bears and penguins,
and a gang of monkeys, too.

They roared and chirped and chattered,
and they put up quite a fuss.
The animals all shouted,
"Come back and live with us!"

The snow dude raced around the park
and up to Snowboard Hill,
the place where all the boys and girls
come out to test their skill.

He grabbed somebody's snowboard
and he rode it like a pro—
leaving everyone behind him
in a frozen spray of snow!

He shot straight down the hillside,
from the summit to the base,
and every little kid in town
was quick to join the chase.

"Please," the children hollered,
"little snow dude, say you'll stay!
Teach us all the tricks you know
and never go away!"

He answered, "I'm a snow dude,
as wild as wild can be.
Run as fast as you can run—
you won't catch up with me!"

A giant crowd had gathered
when the snow dude reached the lake.
He stepped out on the ice, but paused,
afraid that it might break.

Nick and Kara quickly pushed
their way up to the front.
"Listen," Kara hollered,
"we can all get what we want!"

DANGER
THIN ICE!

Magic sparkled in the air—
the wind began to moan.
"It's very simple, everyone:
build snow dudes of your own!"

The snow dude leaped, and clapped his hands,
and all the people smiled,
letting their imaginations
run completely wild.

They stacked and scraped and shaped the snow,
and it was no surprise
that soon the park was filled
with dudes of every shape and size.

The men and women chased them,
and the children laughed with glee
to see the snow dudes playing,
just as happy as could be.

"Will you get what you wish for?"
cried a gust of wind. "Who knows?
For there's a little mischief waiting . . .
every time it snows!"

For Ivy

First Edition
10 9 8 7 6 5 4 3 2 1

Printed in Hong Kong
This book is set in Optima.
Reinforced binding

ISBN 0-7868-1942-1
Library of Congress Cataloging-in-Publication Data on file.

Visit www.hyperionbooksforchildren.com